Great Standards

Seventeen best-loved songs from any era.
Arranged for piano/vocal with chord names and full lyrics.

Amsco Publications
New York • London • Sydney

Front cover photography by David Spindel/SuperStock

This book Copyright © 1995 by Amsco Publications,
A Division of Music Sales Corporation, New York

All rights reserved. No part of this book may be reproduced in any form or by any
electronic or mechanical means, including information storage and retrieval systems,
without permission in writing from the publisher.

Order No. AM 934362
US International Standard Book Number: 0.8256.1528.3
UK International Standard Book Number: 0.7119.5405.4

Exclusive Distributors:
Music Sales Corporation
257 Park Avenue South, New York, New York 10010 USA
Music Sales Limited
8/9 Frith Street, London W1V 5TZ England
Music Sales Pty. Limited
120 Rothschild Street, Rosebery, Sydney, NSW 2018, Australia

Printed and bound in the United States of America by
Vicks Lithograph and Printing Corporation

Angel Eyes *4*

Blue Champagne *7*

But Beautiful *10*

Darn That Dream *14*

Everything Happens To Me *18*

Heartaches *22*

Here's That Rainy Day *24*

Imagination *30*

Let's Get Away From It All *62*

Like Someone In Love *27*

Oh! You Crazy Moon *34*

Polka Dots And Moonbeams *44*

Satin Doll *48*

Swinging On A Star *39*

That's My Desire *52*

There Are Such Things *56*

There, I've Said It Again *59*

Angel Eyes

by Matt Dennis and Earl Brent

Copyright © 1946 (Renewed) by Music Sales Corporation (ASCAP)
International Copyright Secured. All Rights Reserved.

Blue Champagne

by Grady Watts, Jimmy Eaton and Frank Ryerson

Copyright © 1941 (Renewed) by Music Sales Corporation (ASCAP)
International Copyright Secured. All Rights Reserved.

Heartaches

by Al Hoffman and John Kilmer

Copyright © 1931 (Renewed) by Al Hoffman Songs, Inc. (ASCAP) and Leeds Music Corp.
International Copyright Secured. All Rights Reserved.

Here's That Rainy Day

by Johnny Burke and Jimmy Van Heusen

Copyright © 1953 (Renewed) by Music Sales Corporation (ASCAP) and Bourne Co.
International Copyright Secured. All Rights Reserved.

Like Someone In Love

by Johnny Burke and Jimmy Van Heusen

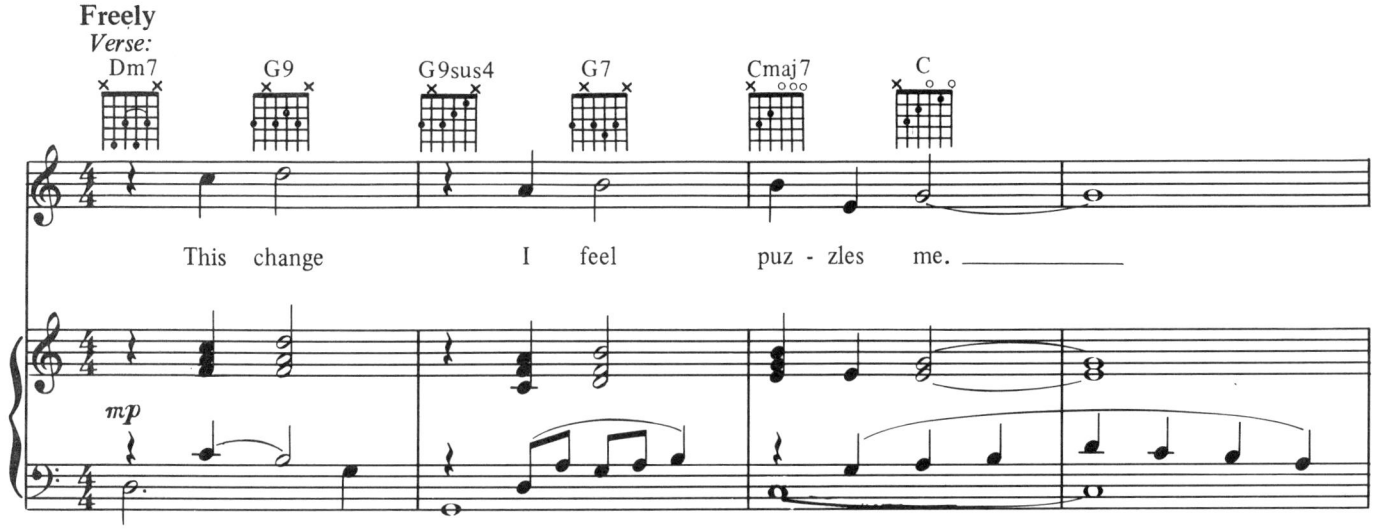

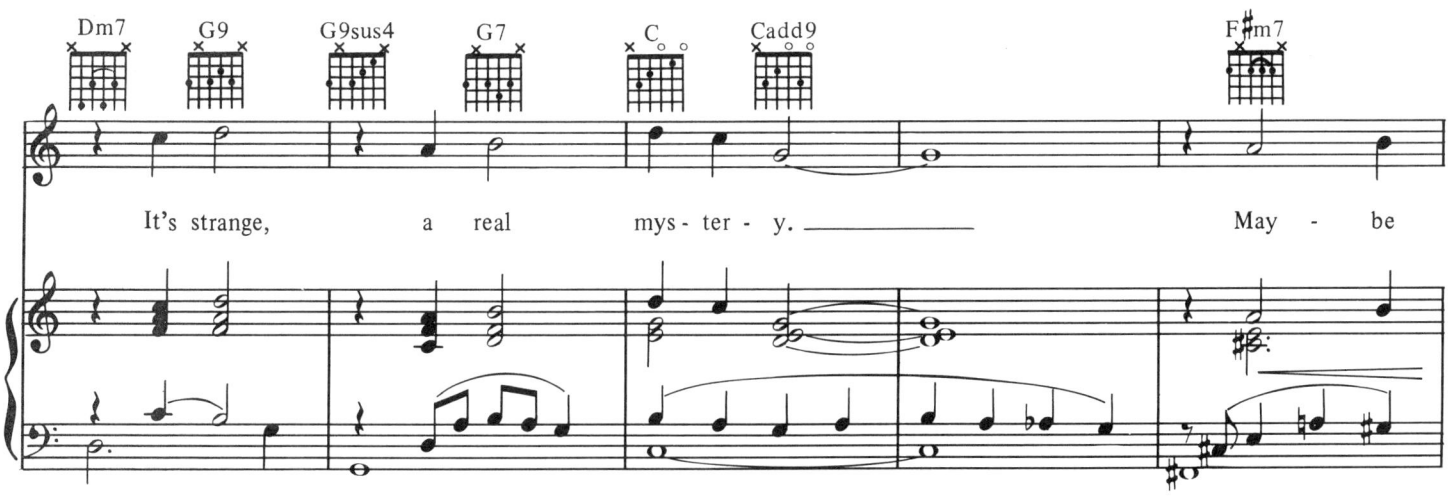

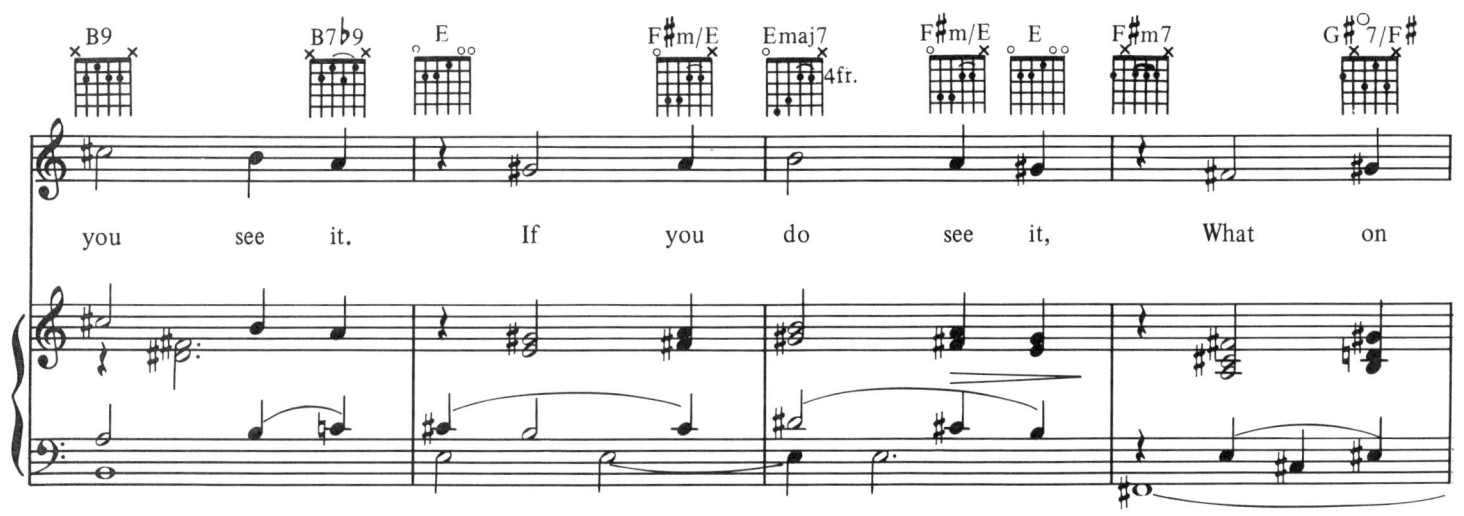

Copyright © 1944 (Renewed) by Music Sales Corporation (ASCAP) and Bourne Co.
International Copyright Secured. All Rights Reserved.

Imagination
by Johnny Burke and Jimmy Van Heusen

Copyright © 1939 (Renewed) by Music Sales corporation (ASCAP) and Bourne Co.
International Copyright Secured. All Rights Reserved.

A7 B♭°7 Am7 D9 G C9
5 fr.
4 fr.
Oh! You craz - y moon, look what you've done!
C♯m7♭5 F♯7 Bm G9♯11 F♯9+ F♯7♭9
Once you prom - ised me, you know, _ that
Bm Bm7 E9 E9♭5 E9 Am
it would nev - er end, You should be a -
F9♯11 E9+ E7♭9 A7 Am7/D D9
4 fr.
shamed to show _ your fun - ny face, my friend.

Am7 D9 Am7 D9 G6 C9
There they are, they fell in love, I guess you think you're
Bm7♭5 E7 A7 B♭°7 Am7 D9
smart Oh! You craz - y moon, you broke my
1. G E♭9♯11 D7♭9♯5 2. G
heart. heart,
F9 A♭9 Gmaj7
You broke my heart.
ritard. e cresc.
f
5 fr.
4 fr.

Swinging On A Star

by Johnny Burke and Jimmy Van Heusen

Moderately, with a bounce

Would you like to swing on a star, Carry moon-beams home in a jar, _____ And be bet-ter off than you

Copyright © 1944 (Renewed) by Music Sales Corporation (ASCAP) and Bourne Co.
International Copyright Secured. All Rights Reserved.

are, Or would you rather be a mule? A mule is an animal with long funny ears, He kicks up at anything he hears. His back is brawny and his brain is weak, He's just plain stupid with a stubborn streak. And by the way, if you hate to go to

A pig is an animal with dirt on his face, His shoes are a terrible disgrace. He's got no manners when he eats his food, He's fat and lazy and extremely rude. But if you don't care a feather or a

school,
You may grow up to be a mule.
fig,
You may grow up to be a pig. Or would you like to swing on a star, Carry moon-beams home in a jar, And be better off than you are, Or would you rather be a pig? A fish. A

fish won't do an-y-thing but swim in a brook, He can't write his name or read a book. ____ To fool the peo-ple is his on-ly thought, ___ And though he's slip-per-y, he still gets caught. But then if that sort of life is what you wish, You may grow up to be a fish. ____ And all the

G7sus4 G7 G9 C7 G♭7♭5 F7sus4 F7 F9
mon - keys aren't in the zoo, Ev - 'ry day you meet quite a
B♭ E♭m6 B♭ A♭7♭5 3 fr. G7sus4 G7 G9 C7
few. So you see it's all up to you.
F9sus4 F9 A♭7♭5 3 fr. G7 Cm7 Gm/D E♭6
You can be bet - ter than you are, You could be
poco a poco cresc.
F9sus4 F7 F7/A B♭ E♭6/B♭ G♭7/B♭ 4 fr. B♭ 6 fr.
swing - ing on a star.
f

Polka Dots And Moonbeams

by Johnny Burke and Jimmy Van Heusen

Slowly, with expression
Chorus:

say it could-n't be true. A coun-try dance was be-ing held in a gar-den, I felt a bump and heard an "Oh, beg your par-don," Sud-den-ly I saw pol-ka dots and moon-beams all a-round a pug-nosed dream. The mus-ic start-ed and was I the per-plexed one,

F
Dm7
5fr.
Gm7
A7+
5 fr.
A7
5fr.
Dm
B♭m6/D♭
3fr.
I held my breath and said "May I have the next one," In my fright-ened arms
F/C
Am7
A♭m7
Gm7
C7♭9
F
E7
pol - ka dots and moon-beams spark - led on a pug-nosed dream. There were
Amaj7
B♭°7
Bm7
Bm7♭5
E7
A
F♯m
3
ques - tions in the eyes of oth - er danc-ers As we float - ed o - ver the
Bm7
E7
A
B♭°7
Bm7
Bm7♭5
E7
floor. There were ques - tions, but my heart knew all the an-swers,

Lyrics:

And per-haps a few things more. Now in a cot-tage built of li-lacs and laugh-ter, I know the mean-ing of the words, "ev-er af-ter." And I'll al-ways see pol-ka dots and moon-beams when I kiss the pug-nosed dream.

Satin Doll

Music by Duke Ellington, Words by Billy Strayhorn and Johnny Mercer

Moderately, with a beat

Cig - a - rette hold - er which wigs me ov - er her should - er, she digs me

Copyright © 1958, 1960 (Renewed) by Tempo Music, Inc./Music Sales Corporation (ASCAP), Famous Music Corp. and Warner Bros. Music Corp.
All rights outside the U.S. controlled by Music Sales Corporation (ASCAP) on behalf of Tempo Music, Inc.
International Copyright Secured. All Rights Reserved.

out catin' that Satin Doll. Baby shall we go out skippin' careful amigo, you're flippin' Speaks Latin

A♭m7 D♭7♭9 C D9 G7♭9 C
that Sat - in Doll. She's
Gm7 C7 Gm7 C7
no - bo - dy's fool, so I'm play - ing it cool as can be,
F Am7 D7
I'll give it a whirl, but I
Am7 D7 G7 Dm7 G7
ain't for no girl catch - ing me.
(Spoken:) Swich - e - Roo - ney

51

That's My Desire

by Caroll Loveday and Helmy Kresa

Slow swing

To spend one night with you in our old rendezvous, and rem-i-

Copyright © 1931 (Renewed) by Music Sales Corporation (ASCAP) and Mills Music EMI
International Copyright Secured. All Rights Reserved.

Em7
Em7/A
A7+
5fr.
Dmaj9
5fr.
Bm
nisce with you, That's my de - sire.
G6add2/A
N.C.
Dmaj9
5fr.
F°7
To meet where gyp - sies play, down in
Em9
7fr.
Em9/A
5fr.
Em9
7fr.
F°7
Em9
7fr.
Em9/A
5fr.
that dim ca - fe, and dance 'til the break of day,
E♭7
6fr.
D
5fr.
E♭9♯11
6fr.
D
5fr.
That's my de - sire. We'll sip a

lit - tle glass of wine___ and I'll___ gaze___ in to your eyes di - vine.___

Instrumental

I'll___ feel a touch of___ your lips press - ing on mine.

To hear you___ whis - per low___ just when_ it's time to go,___ "Che - rie, I love___ you so.___

E♭7
6fr.
D
5fr.
Gm7
Fmaj9
8fr.
E♭maj9♯11
6fr.
Dmaj9
5fr.
D.S. al Coda
3
You're my de - sire."
Coda
F°7
Em9
7fr.
Em9/A
5fr.
"Che - rie, I love you so.
3
Asus4add6
N.C.
D
5fr.
Asus4add6
N.C.
You're my de - sire.
You're my de -
B♭maj7
6fr.
A♭maj7
4fr.
Fm7
8fr.
E♭maj7
6fr.
Dmaj13♯11
5fr.
rit.
sire."
rit.
a tempo

There Are Such Things

by Stanley Adams, Abel Baer and George W. Myer

You may laugh a-bout Thanks - giv-ing, You may think life is wrong;

But you'll find there's joy in liv-ing, When love comes a - long.

Copyright © 1942 (Renewed) by Music Sales Corporation (ASCAP)
International Copyright Secured. All Rights Reserved.

REFRAIN
(Guitar tacet)
a tempo

A heart that's true, _____ there are such things; A dream for two, _____ there are such things; Some-one to whisper, "Darling, you're my guid-ing star;" _____ Not car-ing what you own _____ but just what you are. _____ A peace-ful sky, _____

C7 C+ F6 G7 Dm7
there are such things; A rain-bow high
B7 E7 E7(b5) A7 Dm F6 Fm6
Where heav - en sings; So have a lit-tle faith and trust in
C C7 B7 E7 A7 Bb7 A7 D7
what to - mor - row brings, You'll reach a star be-
G11 G7 G11 G7 1. C Am7 Dm7 G7 (Guitar tacet) 2. C
cause there are such things. A heart that's things.
poco rall
8

There, I've Said It Again

by Redd Evans and Dave Mann

I think I've talked too much al-rea-dy,___ yet the words con-tin-ue to flow. And when I place them all to-geth-er___ they still seem to say "I love you so."___ I've said it.___ What

more can I say? Be-lieve me, there's no oth-er way. I love you no use to pre-tend. There! I've said it a-gain. I've said it. There's no-thing to hide. It's bet-ter than burn-ing in-side. I love you. I will to the end. There! I've said it a-gain. I've tried to drum up a phrase that would sum up all that I feel for you. But what good are phrases? The thought that a-maz-es is you love me, and it's hea-ven-ly. For-give me for want-ing you so, but one thing I want you to know, I've loved you since hea-ven knows when. There! I've said it a-gain. I've

Let's Get Away From It All

by Matt Dennis and Tom Adair

[Verse]
I'm so tired of this dull routine. Up to town on the eight fifteen. Back at night, off to bed and then get up and start it all over again.

[Chorus]
Let's take a boat to Bermuda, Let's take a plane to Saint Paul

Copyright © 1940 (Renewed) by Music Sales Corporation (ASCAP)
International Copyright Secured. All Rights Reserved.

Let's take a kay-ak to Quin-cy or Ny-ack, Let's get a-way from it all.

Let's take a trip in a trail-er No need to come back at all

Let's take a pow-der to Bos-ton for chow-der,

Let's get a-way from it all. We'll tra-vel 'round from

Eb/Bb C7 Fm Bb13 Bb9+ Eb Ebmaj7 Eb6 Edim Bb/F G7(b9)
town to town, We'll vis - it ev - 'ry state I'll re - peat "I
Cm F9 Bb7 Bbdim Bb7 Bb9+ Eb Bb7(b9)
love you, Sweet!" In all the for - ty eight. Let's go a - gain to Ni - a -
Eb7 Ab Adim Eb Fm Bb7
- g'ra this time we'll look at the "Fall" Let's leave our hut, Dear, Get
1 2
Db9 C+ C7 F7 E9 Eb6 Gbdim Fm7 Bb7 Eb6 Bm Eb
out of our rut, Dear, Let's get a - way from it all.